ZOEY

A Novelette by Yvonne N. Pierre

ZOEY

Copyright © 2015 by Yvonne N. Pierre

An imprint of Zyonair's Unlimited, LLC

Synopsis: ZOEY is a very sweet and sensitive portrait of a woman, Claire Harper, who is troubled, confused and angry. Her loving and patient husband tries to make her realize that she is the source of her own unhappiness, but Claire refuses to accept that responsibility. Zoey, the couple's four-year-old daughter, was born with Down syndrome and ever since then Claire has not truly been able to relate to Zoey and her disability. Instead, she chooses to block the truth from her life, won't seek help, and is unable to give Zoey the love she deserves. But when the moment comes that forces Claire to deal with a life-threatening event, she finally realizes the importance of loving her child and her husband and receiving their love in return.

ISBN-13: 978-0692663431

ISBN-10: 0692663436

Categories Fiction, Drama, Short Story, Family, Inspirational

Writers Guild of America Registration #1286347

Edited by Ann K. Fisher

Cover and Interior designs by Yvonne N. Pierre

Biography Photo by Tammy McGarity Photography

CHAPTER
ONE

There are moments that make you question everything. It forces you to take a look at yourself. It challenges what you believe. Moments that brings you to your knees. I like to call them *awakening* moments. We all have them. The question is do you run or do you face it?

The accident was a year ago, but I remember it as if it were yesterday. I felt like I was losing everything - a rug was being snatched from under my feet. I could no longer sit in comfort. I felt like life was being sucked out of me. No one deserves to spend a lifetime not knowing what love, true love, feels like.

The day before the accident, the alarm went off and I jumped out of bed thinking I had overslept. I glanced at the clock. It was 7:00 a.m. I was relieved that I still had an hour and a half before I had to be at work. I noticed David was not in bed, but I assumed that he took Zoey to school. Maybe he was rushing and just forgot to wake me up. I put on my housecoat and grabbed the clothes for work that I had laid out the night before. As soon as I opened the bedroom door to go into the hallway bathroom I smelled bacon and eggs. I heard Zoey, my daughter, laughing downstairs. They hadn't left yet.

I ran downstairs and there was Zoey, all smiles and playing with my mom. But the tension I felt from David was so thick it demanded my attention. He looked at me as if I was his enemy and not his wife. How did we get to this place? It had been brewing for some time. I ignored it because I was angry. I thought things would work themselves out. I guess I was wrong. I didn't want him to leave without us talking this out, but I was too afraid to ask him to stay. I reached to grab his arm. He snatched it away from me. He tried to play it off like he was moving his arm to straighten his tie. It was obvious; he was falling out of love with me. He reached around me and grabbed Zoey's coat from the kitchen chair. It's funny how quickly a relationship can change when you stop speaking from your heart and start speaking from your hurt. I was always defensive.

"David, why didn't you wake me up?"

"Your alarm went off. You're up," David said sarcastically.

I didn't know why he was angry, but it was starting to piss me off. My heart and pride were at war, my pride would often win. I am not going to kiss up to him.

"DAVID! Why didn't you wake me up like you always do?"

He just looked at me, and then began to take Zoey out of her highchair and put her coat on.

"David!" He exhaled as if I was getting on his nerves. "David, you're not going to answer me?"

"Wake you up early so we can do this, Claire? Argue and we go to work angry. Claire, I'm tired of this.   I know you're going through a lot, but I am too. I'm tired of being silent while you mistreat our daughter…"

"Mistreat!" I was hurt. And angry.

David gave me a cold stare and said, "Yes, you act like she's invisible. We've been having this same conversation for four years. Most people don't even know you're a mother."

"David, that's NOT true." I felt an overwhelming sadness. "Okay, maybe it is true; I just don't want people to look down on her. I don't like when people stare."

David clenched his teeth, "I have to go," he said.

"David, what are you saying?"

"I need some space, Claire. We *need* some space."

"All this over some damn social media!"

"Claire, you think all this is about social media? All you care about is what people think of Zoey. No." David zipped up Zoey's coat and grabbed his. "No. Correction: all you care about is what people think of you."

David looked at me and shook his head, "I'm going to stay at my mom's for a couple days. I'm taking Zoey with me."

I was trying to hand him Zoey's backpack before he walked out the door with her, but he snatched it out of my hand. David picked Zoey up in his arms and gave her a kiss on the cheek as he pulled her hood over her head. He grabbed his briefcase and walked out the front door without uttering another word.

He's got me all wrong, I thought. If he wants to stay at his mom's house and not work things out with me, then go right ahead. Maybe he's just looking for something or someone to be mad at. Whatever, I'm not going to chase after him.

I made some coffee and just stood there, confused. My mom looked at me with disappointment and shook her head. I felt like everyone was coming down on me. I went upstairs to get dressed for work. I was about to walk into the bedroom when I caught a whiff of David's cologne. For a moment, I wanted to pick up the phone and call him, but my pride kicked in. I looked over at his side of the bed and his wedding ring caught my eye. It was lying on the nightstand. This took me by surprise. No matter how much we had disagreed, we'd never taken off our rings. Maybe he just forgot. I shook it off and went into the bathroom.

"Claire, what's going on?" my mom wanted to know.

Not wanting to talk about it, I began brushing my teeth, and then I washed my face.

"I don't want to talk about it, Mom."

"I'm sure you don't, but at some point, you're going to have to.

Don't you think you're wrong? David loves his daughter and he was right. How many people know you have a daughter? How many of them know she has Down syndrome? God…"

"Oh my God, mom, I don't want to talk about it. Not right now."

"Remember when you met David? What made you fall in love with him?"

I couldn't avoid it. I began to think back to when we met five years ago.

I walked into the office building. It was beautiful all glass building. I remember getting off of the elevator and walking up to the receptionist desk. The reception-

ist smiled at me when I approached. I smiled back and said, "Good morning, I'm here to see Mr. Harper."

"And who may I say is here to see him?" she asked.

"Tell him Claire Williams from Marketing Plus is here to see him."

She directed me to have a seat in the lobby and I was so in awe of how beautiful the office was that I was hoping that this was my next client.

As soon as I sat down, a tall attractive man walked over to me. My heart was beating fast as I saw him walking towards me. I was expecting him to be an older, unattractive man. I tried to play it off as he reached out his hand to shake mine. He smelt good. He was clean cut and when he opened his mouth to say, "Ms. Williams?" I thought I was going to melt. I slowly lifted my head and replied as if I didn't see him.

My heart was beating so fast. He said again, "Ms. Williams from Marketing Plus." I took a deep breath, looked up at him and smiled. I stood up to shake his hand. "Right this way," he said pointing me in the direction of his office. He let me walk in front of him. I could feel his eyes undressing me. I was sharp. I had just got my hair done. Simple just parted down the middle and straight a little past my shoulders. I wore a form- fitting, professional business pants suit I just bought on sale. I acted like I was making sure I didn't leave anything on the chair, so I looked back and caught him checking me out. I was hoping he was single. I almost forgot why I was there.

I looked over at the receptionist who was shaking her head and smiling at both of us. He ran ahead to open the door for me.

I entered his office. He told me to have a seat. As he walked around to sit at his desk, I was so focused on him that I almost missed the chair. We both laughed. He asked me to call him David right before he asked me out on a date. We soon became inseparable. We would just sit and talk and laugh for hours. It was like we were teenagers. We became the best of friends. Six months later David and I were married.

I wanted to make it right between us, but I was too stubborn. My chest felt tight like there was cotton in my throat. "Mom..." I turned to tell her that I needed to get ready, but she had already left. I smiled and finished getting dressed.

CHAPTER
TWO

I arrived at work twenty minutes early as always. I went into the break room, sat down my laptop bag and went to fix myself a cup of coffee. I stood there in a daze as I poured the coffee into my favorite coffee mug. A co-worker walked into the break room with her little girl. She had just started working here. I smiled at them. The little girl was three years old, a year younger than my daughter. I watched her interact with her mom and I wanted to cry. I wanted Zoey to do those things. Zoey was four years old and still learning how to run without falling. I was happy for my co-worker, but the more I saw kids doing what Zoey couldn't do, the sadder I became.

I wiped a tear from my eye as I grabbed my coffee and headed to my office. I opened the door and reached over to turn the light on. The first thing I saw was the mountain of work on my desk. I didn't realize until that moment that everything had piled up. I was suddenly overwhelmed. Avoiding what I didn't want to do, well, it had finally caught up with me. For weeks, I was doing enough to stay busy but I wasn't getting anything done. All of a sudden, I had a headache and I felt sick.

My office phone rang, but I didn't have the energy to speak to anyone. I didn't even look at the phone to see who was calling. The phone rang again, but I just turned around and gazed out the window. Snow had begun to fall. I was trying not to feel or think of anything. I just watched the falling snow. My stare out the window was interrupted by a knock on my office door. Without even turning around, I just said, "Come in." I still stood there with my arms crossed looking out of the window. "Are you okay?" a man asked. It was my boss. After he came in, I sat down and offered him a seat.

"Hi, Blake. What brings you to my office?"

"Claire, you've been working with us for a long time…"

"Wait…"

At this point, I was ready for anything. Although I loved my job, I knew I hadn't been productive. I felt defeated.

"This is not starting off well. Are you firing me?"

"No, Claire, I am not firing you. I am giving you some time off. You've been through a lot in the past few weeks and I think you just need a couple of weeks off. Don't worry about your accounts. I will bring a temp in to keep everything up to date."

I had been trying to be tough and not show emotion, but I just broke down crying. Yes, I need some time off. I was to a breaking point and I'm glad Blake saw that instead of firing me. He stood up and walked over to the side of my desk. I turned to face him, still crying. He grabbed my hands and told me everything was going to be okay.

"Claire, you are one of the best workers I have. You are amazing at what you do. But right now everything that is going on with you personally is affecting your work here. You've built relationships with clients that stay with us because of you. Take some time. Come back re-freshed. Okay?"

I was relieved as I wiped the tears from my eyes.

"Thank you, Blake."

I stood up and gave him a hug. He squeezed my hand and walked out of the office. I grabbed a Kleenex from the box on my desk, wiping my tears and trying not to smear my makeup. I took a deep breath, got my things and turned the office light off.

On my way home, all I could think of was my argument with David. I'm not much of a drinker, but I stopped by the liquor store and bought a six-pack of coolers, a 40-ounce bottle of beer and a pint of gin. And some ice cream. I needed something to get my mind off of things. My heart was hurting and I didn't want to feel that. I didn't want to face or talk about anything. I just wanted to drink enough to make me sleep.

When I arrived home my mom greeted me at the door.

"Why are you home so early?" She asked with a worried look on her face.

"I was given some time off."

"What's in the paper bag, Claire?"

My mom looked at me as if I had probably lost my mind.

"Mom…"

"So, Claire, this is how you're going to deal with things, by not dealing with them?"

"MOM! Oh my God, just let me be. Please!"

I tried to ignore her as I took my coat and shoes off. But she wouldn't let it go. I know she wants the best for me. I know that she loves her granddaughter, but I just didn't want to deal with it at that moment. I just wanted to get drunk, eat my ice cream and go to bed. But mom wasn't going to let it go.

"Claire, things are not going to get better unless you talk about it."

I just leaned against the kitchen counter and begged, "Mom! Please let up."

"David is obviously upset about how you're treating Zoey. So, Claire, what is your issue with a four-year-old?"

"Okay." I closed my eyes and surrendered. "Okay. I don't know... I don't know HOW to love her. I'm afraid. I can't seem to see past her disability. Mom, I'm so scared."

Without a response, she left again. I wanted her to tell me what to do. How do I deal with this? But I guess it's for me to understand and sort out. All these years, I never thought about it. I just went through the motions. When did I stop living and just go through the motions? Well, I'll deal with it later. Right now, I'm just going to sit here, eat my ice cream, watch TV and drink.

CHAPTER THREE

The phone rang. I jumped up. The ring of my cell phone startled me. I was in a deep sleep. I'm a little mad. I was just about to meet Prince, in my dream. When I opened my eyes, I was surrounded by empty bottles, empty potato chip bags, an ice cream container and a spoon with peanut butter stuck to my leg. I had a pounding headache. My leg and neck were cramped. Oh my God, what have I done?

I stumbled upstairs to see why David didn't wake me. I noticed some of his things were gone including his suitcase. I went into Zoey's room and realized some of her stuff was missing too. I got angry all over again. My cell phone rang again. It was David's mother. I put the phone in my pocket. David wanted some space and wanted to stay with his mom. She always called when David and I got into an argument. I didn't feel like talking to my own mother - I damn sure didn't want to talk to his. I was hoping she would just leave a message, but she didn't. The phone rang again. It's like she was hanging up and hitting redial. I just kept hitting the side button to silence it. I hate ignoring her calls, but I just didn't feel like talking about it.

"Oh my God, Claire look at this mess," my mom said.

I pretended I didn't hear her. I went downstairs to get some water. The phone rang again. I took it out of my pocket and just stared at it wondering if I should answer it. My mom gave me "the look" without saying a word. So, I answered.

"Heeello."

"Claire?"

"Yes, ma'am it's me."

"I've been trying to call you since last night... David and

Zoey never made it to my house. They were in an accident..."

From that point forward, every word she said sounded muffled. It was all a blur. I just remember her telling me what hospital. I dropped the phone and stood there in shock. My mouth fell open. My knees felt like they were about to buckle. I looked over at my mom, grabbed my keys, and threw on my shoes and coat. I couldn't move fast enough. It was all happening in slow motion. When I got outside, I turned to lock the door and rushed to the car. It had snowed last night. I had to let the car warm up while I scraped the windows so I could see. When I finally backed out I noticed the streets weren't too bad, they must have put salt down. I felt overwhelmed. "Oh my God, traf-fic," I said aloud.

CHAPTER
FOUR

I never like Chicago traffic, but to-day I hated it. Every light felt like 20 minutes and it was bumper to bumper traffic. I wanted to run every stop sign and traffic light. I just want to get there. Maybe I needed this time to think. I kept deep breathing to calm myself. I looked over at my mom who had this "now do you have time to talk about it" look on her face. I was caught by a red light. I guess I couldn't run anymore.

Four years ago, when I was pregnant with Zoey, David and I were so excited. We were having our first baby. It was during a time when we were so in love. He was excited to the point he sort of got on my nerves. The doctor asked if we wanted to have the amniocentesis test to see if the baby had a disability or not. David didn't want the test, but I did. I didn't want a child that wasn't normal. It didn't matter to David and that's when we began to have issues. I had the test. It came back positive; I was far into the pregnancy and considered adoption. I didn't want my child to live a life of challenges, being judged or treated unfairly. My excitement at having a baby changed. I became depressed.

When Zoey was born, I cried. I felt so sorry for her. I questioned what I did wrong. I questioned if David did something wrong. I questioned everything. How could He do this to us? How could He do this to an innocent child? Why couldn't I have a normal child? I was angry at God. How could this happen to us?

Over the years, David and I began to grow apart. He wanted me to be as involved as he was, but I just couldn't. So, I didn't. When Zoey's physical, speech and occupational therapists would arrive, David would sit there excited and asked questions about how we can help her. I tried to be present, but I started to pull away from them both. I began to resent David. We began to argue about everything. Looking back, 99% of it was unnecessary arguments, really silly arguments over him leaving something on the sink and I took it personally as if he left it for me to clean up. Instead of me dealing with what I was feeling, everything got under my skin. I focused on hurt. I didn't realize I was creating more pain for myself and misery for those around me.

I looked up and realized we were almost at the hospital. But we were caught by another light. I turned and looked at my mother and began to weep. It all hit me, everything that I did wrong. My heart began to feel heavy. The tears flowed. I felt anxious about David,

Zoey, and my mom. I kept looking at her, thinking about how much I missed her physical presence. My mom passed away a couple weeks before Zoey was born, which pushed me into an early labor. Zoey was born on my mother's birthday, March 21. Mom is forever my guardian angel.

> "My God! Please don't take them away from me. Give me a chance to get it right."

At the hospital, I parked the car, but before I got out, I had to take a moment to pull myself together. I looked over at my mom and broke down crying.

> "Mom, I miss you. I can't lose them, too."

> "I miss you too, Claire."

"I don't know what to do."

"You go in there and find out what's going on."

I nodded, "Mom, I wish I could hold you again."

"I wish I could hold you, too. Claire, you have to live on. You can't live your life afraid of getting too close because you're afraid of losing. It's not fair to Zoey and David that your fear prevents you from loving. God is not pushing you. Zoey is a gift packaged differently. She needs you. She needs all of you. You gotta live. A major part of living is loving. Your problem is you're too focused on what is wrong; you're missing all that is right. I'll always be here for you, Claire."

I couldn't breathe I was crying so hard, "Lord, take the wheel" I kept repeating to myself. She was right. I took a deep breath, wiped away my tears, jumped out of the car and ran into the hospital.

CHAPTER
FIVE

I ran up to the receptionist desk. I was so overwhelmed I couldn't get my thoughts straight.

I took a very deep breath and said, "I'm here to see two patients: Zoey and David Harper."

The receptionist clicked keys on her computer, and then said to me, "Mr. Harper has been re-leased. Zoey is in ICU."

She asked me to sign in and handed me a pass. I rushed off, but as soon as I turned the corner I saw a chapel. I need-ed to say a quick prayer before checking on Zoey. I stood in the doorway afraid to go in. I was overwhelmed with guilt and terrified of losing Zoey. My throat was dry and my chest felt tight.

When I walked into the chapel, Da-vid was sitting there on his knees crying out to God. I didn't want to interrupt, so I stood there not knowing how to re-spond, not knowing what to say to my own husband. I had spent so much time trying to do it my way; it was time for me to do it His way. I closed my eyes and asked God to guide me. In fact, I had a long talk with God as I stood there. I apologized for not trusting Him and His will for me. I apologized to God for being angry at Him, for taking my mother, and angry about Zoey having Down syndrome. I could taste the tears streaming into my mouth.

David noticed me. He stood up and turned to face me. He stood there with tears in his eyes. He had a brace on his arm and a big bruise on his face. He began to limp toward me. I just stood there. He hugged me and I could feel him letting go of being upset. I let go, too. It seemed like we just stood there holding each other for hours. I didn't want to let go. I felt safe.

"Have you been to see Zoey already?"

"No, I came here first."

He nodded and said, "She's resting."

"What happened?"

"I came home to talk to you about us working things out, but you were knocked out. When I tried to wake you, you pushed me away and told me to get out. The house was a mess; I could tell you'd been drinking. So, I grabbed Zoey and some things to stay at my mom's house for a few days. When I left, it was snowing - they hadn't cleaned the roads yet.

I looked into the rearview mirror and saw Zoey laughing and playing. It looked like she was talking to someone next to her. I smiled. You know Zoey loves to sing and dance. I turned the radio on and we began to sing. As I was looking at Zoey, I noticed the light turned green. So, I began to drive. The car facing me must have hit an ice patch. It went into a spin and hit me on the driver's side. The impact was so hard my window and the dash window was shattered, I went into a spin. I wasn't worried about me. I tried to control the car. From that point on, it's all a blur. I remember flashing lights, police and fire trucks surrounding the streets. I remember being on a gurney, rushed into the hospital. I remember them taking Zoey and I tried to reach for her and I guess I blanked out." David cried and closed his eyes. He put his head on my shoulder. "The driver that hit us died."

I began to weep. "Oh my God, David, I am so, so sorry. The thought of losing you… I'm sorry for everything. I'm going to do better."

I stood up, took a deep breath, reached out my hand and said, "Let's go see Zoey." David stood up, looked me in the eye and I could feel his love for me. I closed my eyes to take it in. It felt so good. We left the chapel and headed to ICU.

Zoey was asleep and the presence of my mom and God filled the room. David sat down and I stood by Zoey's bed. She had a breathing tube down her throat and bruises everywhere. I grabbed her hand. She looked so beautiful. It was as if I was seeing her for the first time. Her eyes. I love her slanted pretty eyes. I didn't want her to see me cry, but I couldn't hold back the tears.

The nurse came in and told us she was going to be okay. She didn't have any major injuries. She said that Zoey's going to be in a lot of pain due to the impact, but she was very lucky. They were going to keep her overnight for observation. Her oxygen was slightly low, but the nurse said again, "Mrs. Harper, your little girl is going to be okay." She gave my hand a reassuring squeeze. "The doctor will remove the breathing tubes in the morning."

I exhaled. I'm so grateful that I was given a second chance to show her love. I leaned over and gave her a long kiss on her forehead. She's so beautiful, I thought. I couldn't bear the thought of losing her. I squeezed her hand tightly.

CHAPTER SIX

A couple of weeks later, I was in a deep sleep, but I could hear a faint voice saying, "Ah me. Ah me. Ah me." I opened my eyes and Zoey was standing there, "Ah me... eat, eat." That's how she says mommy. Listening to her speak now is like a melody to my ears. All the times she said it and I wasn't listening.

I looked over at the clock; it was a few minutes before it was set to go off. I looked over at David asleep. Man, oh man. I love that man. We still have disagreements, but the difference is that we're the best of friends. We have each others' best interest at heart. We go on dates. I had begun to take him for granted, but not anymore. We've agreed to be honest with ourselves first and each other about how we feel so we can deal with it as best friends do. We had a talk the other day about Zoey. He explained to me that he was upset that I was denying an important part of him – Zoey. She's his world. I admire my husband's love for his daughter.

I didn't want to wake him yet so I tried to quietly sneak out the room. I put my finger up to my lip, "Shhh, Zoey." She had a surprised look and began to tiptoe too. I wanted to run back and get my phone to record it, but we were almost out the door. When we got downstairs she threw her arms up like we did it. I grabbed her up and gave her a whole bunch of kisses. When I put her down she took off towards the kitchen.

"So, Zoey what do you want for breakfast, sweetheart?"

She pointed at the cereal box.

"No, Zoey use your words. I… want…. cereal." I'd been sitting in her therapy sessions and talking to her therapist to see how I can help Zoey.

"I ant ereal."

"Yes.   Good job." I smiled proudly.

I began to fix her some cereal. She went to turn on the TV and there was a little static. I was about to rush over to help her, but she had already fixed it. She'd been watching her dad fix it. She amazes us daily with all the things she can do. She's like a sponge. She soaks it all in and when I think she isn't paying attention, she proves that she is. The more I pay attention to what she can do, the more I see.

I heard David coming downstairs. He always wants cereal, so I grabbed a bowl for him. He ran over to Zoey and started playing with her, daddy's girl. I love watching them play. I love them so much. I am always crying. But there are not sad tears.

I looked over and my mom was standing there smiling. I was sad because I knew this meant letting her go. I felt a lump in my throat. She waved at Zoey. Zoey waved back, "Bye gamma."

I was sad for a moment, then I realized how blessed I was to have that extra time with my mother. My lips motioned, "Thank you." She nodded and smiled. I could tell she didn't want to leave, but she had to. Her job was done.

Zoey looked at me and then looked at my mom. She noticed what was happening. She stood up and walked over to me and gave me a hug. I needed that.

Then she said clear as day, "It's okay, mom. Better now."

I began to cry and looked at my mom and motioned my lip to say, "I love you, mom." She said, "I love you, too." She turned and walked away.

David looked up and noticed I was crying. "What's wrong?"

"I'm missing my mom."

He stood up and gave me the best full body hug. I felt Zoey's hands around my leg. I looked down and she was hugging one of each of our legs. We both began to laugh.

"I have to get ready for work."

"How does it feel to be promoted to marketing manager?"

I thought about it for a moment. "It feels good. It truly feels amazing."

David smiled. "I'm so proud of you." He gave me a kiss.

"David, I have to get dressed for work." We both giggled.

"Give me a kiss, Zoey."

She ran up to me and gave me a huge hug and kiss.

Although I love my job, I now hate leaving Zoey. I think about her all day at work. I have pictures all over my office and on social media of Zoey, David and me. My heart is full.

CHAPTER
SEVEN

Life has a way of giving us signs to let us know if we're going in the right or wrong direction. Throughout my life, I was pushed, pulled and brought to my knees only to find I was being pointed in the right direction. But I was so focused on what was happening to me, I lost sight of a daughter. I was going through life living how I felt others thought I should, and ashamed of the things that didn't resemble what is acceptable. They say you shouldn't have regrets, but I do. I regret denying my husband and my daughter love. By not allowing myself to love them, I denied being loved.

When I could no longer hear God's whispers, He sent a familiar voice. A voice He knew I could hear clearly, my mother. From time to time, when I need her she's there. When I don't see her, I feel her presence. My mom was right. The other day, Zoey and her dad fell asleep on the couch watching TV. I sat there looking at them both. I cried thinking I would be sad to lose them, but even sadder if they left here without a fair shot at love. David chose me to be his wife and God chose us to be Zoey's parents. I took that for granted because I couldn't see past myself. We still have our disagreements, but we decided to make loving each other a priority in our relationship. That means listening and trying to understand each other's side of the disagreement. I'm open now to compromise, once I realized that it doesn't demolish me to love him. Being true to myself is, to be honest with self and being okay with not having to be right all the time.

I don't care anymore what people think. Well. Wait. Okay, maybe a little, but not to the point where I deny myself or those whom I love. That's another thing Zoey taught me. People are going to judge you regardless. I am blessed and I will not allow anyone ever again distort the view I have for myself. Until my last breath, I will embrace it all. The good and the bad. All the great moments and the challenging ones with Zoey. I'm ready to be all that God has created me to be. No more walls.

Every day Zoey teaches me something different about her abilities, life, God and us. Ultimately, she taught me love – unconditional love. Through seeing beyond her flaws, I learned how to see beyond my own. Life is too fragile to waste it living in fear of living. Things are not perfect, but I will embrace all that life has to offer - the good and the bad. Everything affects everything.

Yes, Zoey has challenges. Her diagnoses are only to inform us what challenges she might face, it's not a description of who she is. There's so much more to Zoey than Down syndrome. I see that now. I often ask God to take the wheel, not realizing He was driving the whole time.

"When you focus on someone's disability you'll overlook their abilities, beauty, and uniqueness. Once you learn to accept and love them for who they are, you subconsciously learn to love yourself unconditionally."

BONUS MATERIALS

WHAT IS
DOWN
SYNDROME?

Down syndrome (Ds) is a genetic condition. The most common form of Down syndrome is often called "trisomy 21," because individuals with this condition have three copies of the 21st chromosome.

Each cell in the human body contains 23 pairs of chromosomes, which contain the genetic material that determines all our inherited characteristics. We receive half of each chromosome pair from our mother and the other half from our father. Individuals with the most common form of Down syndrome, trisomy 21, have an extra 21st chromosome.

No one knows exactly why this chromosomal error occurs, but it does appear to be related to the age of the mother.

With early intervention and health care, individuals with Down syndrome are living longer and happier lives.

In the U.S. today, Down syndrome affects approximately 350,000 people. As many as 80% of adults with this condition reach age 55, and many live longer.

IMPORTANT AWARENESS DATES

March (First Wednesday of the Month)
Spread the Word to End the Word

March 21 - World Down syndrome Awareness Day

October - Down syndrome Awareness Month

FOR MORE INFORMATION AND RESOURCES

National Down syndrome Society -
http://www.ndss.org

Parent to Parent USA (Resource Database)
- http://www.p2pusa.org

Emory University School of Medicine - Department of Human Genetics -
http://genetics.emory.edu/patient-care/down-syndrome-clinic.html

Special Olympics -
http://www.specialolympics.org

VSA Arts - http://education.kennedy-center.org//education/vsa

Buddy Walk - http://www.ndss.org/Buddy-Walk

Best Buddies - https://bestbuddies.org

Buddy Cruise - http://www.buddycruise.org

Parents are a great resource. Be sure to seek parent groups and helpful pages on social media.

YVONNE PIERRE

As a survivor of childhood sexual abuse, rape and the murder of her father as a small child, Yvonne continues to use her gifts to bring about positive change. Yvonne is a proud wife and loving mother of two sons. Her youngest was diagnosed with Down syndrome (Ds) after birth, which ignited her passion for using her voice to make a difference.

Yvonne's journey of advocating positive awareness for Down syndrome starting in 2004 when she launched "Have Ya Heard," an online community that evolved into "HYH Rise Awards" in 2011. The awards were an online event celebrating and honoring those who are making a difference in the Ds community. Her mission is to show the positive side of having a child with special needs. In 2007, she produced and hosted over 100 episodes of her own syndicated talk show "The Yvonne Pierre Show." In 2010, Yvonne wrote an inspirational memoir "The Day My Soul Cried." With the launch of Y Pierre Productions, Yvonne wrote, produced and directed a stage play called "Then You Stand," in 2012. That same year, Yvonne wrote an award-winning short film called, "Never Alone." In 2014, she executive produced "The 2014 Rise Awards" held in Decatur, GA. In 2015, Yvonne wrote a critically-acclaimed musical dramedy stage play called, "It Takes Two." In 2016, she wrote a novelette "Zoey" and "The 2016 Rise Awards" online. "Life is so much bigger than the eyes can see and the heart can feel." Yvonne's passion and purpose are to use the power of storytelling to give hope and provide a different perspective on life.

Connect with Yvonne on:

Facebook.com/writerypierre

Twitter.com/ypierre

Instagram.com/writer_ypierre

About.me/ypierre

www.ingramcontent.com/pod-product-compliance
Lightning Source LLC
Chambersburg PA
CBHW020645130626
46552CB00003B/1402